The WICHT

Chronicles

Fen Gold

by Joan Lennon

ANDERSEN PRESS

First published in Great Britain in 2007
by Andersen Press Limited
20 Vauxhall Bridge Road
London SW1V 2SA
www.andersenpress.co.uk
www.joanlennon.co.uk.

Text © Joan Lennon, 2007
Illustration © David Wyatt, 2007

British Library Cataloguing in Publication Data available.
ISBN 978 184 270 632 9

Printed in the UK by CPI Bookmarque, Croydon, CR0 4TD

To Lindsey, with more gratitude
than would fill a page – A1, even,
and writing very small.

Acknowledgements

I'd like to thank Fraser Ross Associates for being my agents, and the many people at and around Andersen Press who are working so hard to get The Wickit Chronicles out there and looking so good.

Contents

Brother Gilbert

Prior Benet

Brother Barnard

Abbot Michael

Brother John

Brother Paul

Wickit Monastery:

Abbot Michael - the chief monk, the father of the community

Prior Benet - second in command

Brother Gilbert - the Infirmarer - the monk in charge of medical care, including making medicines

Brother Barnard - the Cellarer - the monk in charge of food and provisions

Brother Paul - Wickit's handyman

Brother John

Pip

Perfect

Perfect

Pip

The Norse:

Lady Rane

Haakon - her kinsman

Leif and Olaf - the twins from Helheim

Lady Rane

Haakon

From King Arnald's Court:

Leif and Olaf

Cedric

The Fen People

Sly the fisherman

Fosse the peat-cutter

Ghosts in the Mist

The Fenland has always been a mysterious place, where odd things are more likely to happen than ordinary ones. Old Fisher Sly knew this perfectly well, and so he didn't immediately have a heart attack when he saw, just where the northern marsh meets the sea, a Viking longship gliding past him in the mist. He knew this was impossible – Viking raiders had stopped terrorising the coast over a hundred years ago. So it could only be a ghost ship. That much was certain. Sly had seen lots of ghosts over the years, and knew how to deal with them. The important thing was not *him* seeing *them* – the important thing was making absolutely certain sure *they* didn't see *him*!

11

He waited quietly in the mist a while longer, and then poled carefully away, in the opposite direction . . .

Fosse was not entirely a Fenman. He lived on the southern edges of the great marsh, a sort of half-and-half existence. He was primarily a peat-digger, but when the King's man offered to pay if he'd take him in his boat to Ely, he didn't say no. But then, he hadn't expected the man to fall ill like that . . .

As he punted along through the mist, he was wondering to himself, *What do I do if he dies before I can get him to Ely?! What if they think I murdered him? Who would believe me if I said I didn't? I wonder how much money he has in his belt?* He was not an optimistic man at the best of times, and this journey was beginning to give him the creeps. He was so keyed up he almost fell out of the punt when, without warning, a *thing* came flying out of the fog, right over his head. It looked *exactly* like an airborne stone dragon, and when it caught sight of him, it jinxed sideways with a cry of 'Whoops!' before disappearing again – but of course *that* was *impossible*.

He crossed himself hurriedly, and made the sign against the evil eye as well, just for good measure. The sick man groaned in the bottom of the boat, but his eyes were still tight shut – he wouldn't have seen anything. Fosse noticed he'd thrown off his cloak again, but there was no way he was stopping to cover him up! With a muttered prayer, he dug the punting pole down into the mud and pushed *hard* – only managing to miss the boat that suddenly appeared from the other direction by inches.

'*God's Teeth – where the devil did you pop up from?!*' he yelled.

'Wickit!'

Both boats had done nose-dives into the opposite reed beds, and were now swinging together backwards across the channel. Fosse saw the other punter was only a boy – who was looking at least as scared as *he* felt at the near miss in the mist.

'From Wickit? You're from the Abbey, eh?' Fosse said in a much calmer voice, but before he could ask anything else, the sick man reared up suddenly and croaked, 'Wickit? Wickit?' before collapsing into the bottom of the boat again.

The boy's eyes went even wider, and

his mouth made a round O in his face.

Fosse laughed, feeling superior, and also relieved now he had an answer to his dilemma. 'I've got a strange cargo today, and no mistake! I'm meant to take him to Ely, but Wickit's a lot closer. *That's* where I'll take him, and no blame to me. And I'd like to deliver him soon – the Fever's got into him, as you can see.'

'I can show you the way,' the boy said. 'Follow me!'

It took a bit of flailing and grunting to loosen the mud's hold on the two boats and get them facing the right way round. By the time they were safely underway, Fosse had decided not to mention the 'thing' he thought he'd seen fly over his head. He knew well enough the fog could play tricks with your eyes (he chose not to think about the 'Whoops!' he'd *heard*), and there was no point worrying the lad.

'By the way, boy,' he called to him instead. 'What's your name?'

'Pip,' the answer came back, like a drift of mist. 'I'm Pip.'

Chapter 2

Pip and Perfect

The summer had been long, and hot, and *full* of biting insects, as only a marsh of several thousand square miles can produce. And Pip had been utterly miserable for most of it.

The reason he felt so mouldy was simple – all the excitement of his adventure at Ely that Easter was in the past. There would never be anything like it again. That moment of triumph, as he sang his solo in the most beautiful Lady Chapel in the world – what could ever better that? The hours of cold terror, as he and the young King Arnald struggled to stay alive – when would he ever experience anything as heart-pounding and desperate again?

Pip was back at Wickit for good, and though he loved his home, he knew it was a place where only *ordinary* things happened.

He moped round the abbey with his own personal little black cloud over his head for weeks. Some of the Brothers understood. They could remember what it was like to be Pip's age, and they did their best to keep him out of the way of people like Prior Benet, who couldn't.

'I bet Benet was *born* old and narky,' said Brother Paul, though he was ashamed of himself afterwards.

(The other person the Brothers kept Pip away from during this time was Brother John. This wasn't because he was unpleasant – in fact, Brother John was *so* pleasant and cheerful and relentlessly good-humoured that they were afraid Pip might decide to kick him, out of sheer irritation.

'I know I've wanted to, now and then,' they admitted to each other privately. 'He's a lovely man, but a little can be as good as a feast sometimes.')

So in the days and weeks that followed, instead of an Ely Plot there was a Wickit Conspiracy. Every time Prior Benet's angry bony figure came round a corner, somebody would grab Pip and set him something urgent to do. Brother Paul (who, in spite of having the strength of two other Brothers put together in his wiry, scrawny-looking body, could *not* abide heights) had him re-roofing the outbuildings, after first cutting and bundling the reeds. Brother Barnard the Cellarer was a small man with a large voice, and a face almost the same colour as his curly russet hair, from all those years of cooking for the Abbey at an open hearth. *He* was more than willing to have an assistant for a thousand jobs, from salting fish to smoking ham to brewing beer. And Pip's well-loved Abbot Michael doubled the time they spent together, encouraging and exhorting the boy in his lilting Welsh voice with his singing practice and his Latin lessons. But it was only when Brother Gilbert the Infirmarer got his big blunt hands on Pip that the Conspiracy really started to succeed.

Even when there were no sick people in the Abbey's tiny Infirmary, there was always a lot of work to be done – herbs and flowers and roots and barks needed to be dried and pounded and steeped and boiled, and made into pastes and decoctions and potions and poultices. It could be fiddly work, and mistakes didn't just mean the work needing to be done again. They could be definitely dangerous as well. Something benign and beneficial in one quantity or preparation could be lethal in another. Brother Gilbert was a good man, and a good teacher who loved his work, but he was also an exacting master.

'Saints preserve us – is this going to work?' the Brothers wondered. But it wasn't long before they found out.

Brother Gilbert had just stepped out of the Infirmary for a moment to fetch something. When he returned, he paused in the door-way, and a slow smile spread across his wide, frog-like face. He'd set Pip to grinding ginger in the mortar and for the first time in a long while, the boy was humming at his work! The Conspiracy was a success!

Someone else who was pleased with Pip's new interest was Perfect. She was a quite small gargoyle, made of stone in the shape of a dragon, with claws and wings and a long tail and big eyes.

Pip had found her in amongst the stone leaves and flowers on the tower of Wickit church, where she had been ever since her Maker, the travelling stone carver, Vincenzi, made her all those years ago. Now she and Pip were inseparable friends, and Pip's black time had been hard for her. Things made of stone don't go through stages the way humans do, and she had no way of understanding what was wrong with her boy. And with the Brothers hovering around and giving him jobs to do all the time, she was on the verge of being discovered several times a day.

(Neither Pip nor Perfect knew for certain what would happen if the Brothers of Wickit Abbey – or anybody else, for that matter – found out that part of their fine stone church was alive, fully detachable, and able to fly, swim and talk. They had a pretty good idea it wouldn't be anything good, however, and might very well include being burned at the stake.)

But it wasn't just Pip being *happier* that pleased her.

'I like the room with the smells best,' Perfect announced one evening when she and Pip were alone together.

'What, the *kitchen*?' Pip was surprised – he

thought the kitchen was too noisy and crowded for Perfect's taste – but she shook her head.

'No, the *other* room. I like the way it makes you smell too, when you work there.' She drew a deep breath and closed her eyes. 'Valerian, lavender, red rose, elderflower,' she murmured. 'Lovely.'

Pip was impressed. She was absolutely right. He'd been learning to make different medicines to draw out the pain of headaches that afternoon and Brother Gilbert had had him repeating the ingredients over and over to get them by heart. 'How is it, though, that you can remember all those names,' he wondered, 'when you can't remember Brother Gilbert's name, or Abbot Michael, or Brother Paul?'

Perfect shrugged one small stony shoulder. Scents were vivid and unique. Humans – other than Pip, of course – were pretty much of a muchness. It was *obvious*.

It was some time before it occurred to Pip that having such a skilful herbalist's nose was a bit odd in a creature made of stone.

'I wonder why you're so good at green things – you know, plants and flowers?' he said one day. He was punting very, very slowly on his way to check the Abbey eel traps. There was no point in hurrying. He knew from long experience that there was *never* any shortage of eels, either in the water or on the menu.

Perfect swivelled her head round to look at him. She was in her favourite perch, leaning forward at the very front of the boat, like a pint-sized figurehead.

'My Maker could make me any way he wanted. He obviously wanted me to be like *this*!' She turned back, convinced by her argument.

Pip thought about it some more, and then he was convinced too. He remembered the first time he'd seen Perfect, up in the tower of Wickit church. She'd been surrounded by the most exquisitely carved stone leaves and flowers and fruit. Each detail was delicately, lovingly done. If he hadn't been so busy being amazed by Perfect herself, Pip would have had trouble believing they *were* stone.

Brother Gilbert continued to be extremely pleased with his new apprentice. Pip really was keen, and having a small voice in his hood ready to supply the name of any herb he might forget was a huge help.

Things looked set for being pretty much all right for them both again.

But neither Pip nor Perfect could see into the future. They had no inkling that troubles were already heading, inexorably, towards Wickit from opposite ends of the Fenland. They had no way of guessing just how soon their world was going to change – again!

Chapter 3

The Infirmary Has a Patient

It was just before dawn when the King's man – whose name was Cedric – opened his eyes. By the light of a shielded lantern, he could see he was in some sort of infirmary, small and smelling of medicines and herbs. His fuzzy brain told him he must be in an abbey or a monastery or a nunnery, but he had no idea which one or where.

Just then someone came in. It was a stubby man in a habit and sandals, with a wide, ugly, kindly face and tonsured hair.

'Not a nunnery, then,' murmured the sick man.

The Infirmarer's chuckle was rich and deep.

'Not when I last checked, no,' he said. 'But

it's good news to hear you speaking sense again, more or less. Now drink this.'

Cedric shivered as the monk raised him up and held a cup to his lips. 'Why – what was I saying before?' he asked between sips. The thought that he'd been babbling made him anxious, though he couldn't just at the moment remember why.

'Don't worry – nothing said in my Infirmary ever goes beyond these walls. Safe as the confessional, my son. Have no fear.'

It was as if the word 'fear', spoken out loud, flung open a door in Cedric's mind. He reared up against the Infirmarer's hands.

'My belt – the King – my—'

Brother Gilbert neatly plucked the belt from a stool beside him and thrust it into the man's flailing grasp.

'There now, calmly, calmly. There are no thieves here,' he murmured soothingly.

But Cedric didn't hear him. As soon as his hands assured him that the letters – and the secret reports – sewn into his belt were still there, a reassuring bulge, his mind gave in to the Infirmarer's potion. Before Brother Gilbert had laid him down again on the straw mattress, he was already deep asleep. But even unconscious, he wouldn't let go of his belt, and Brother Gilbert wisely let it be.

When Cedric came to himself again, the monk was gone. Daylight streamed through the open doorway, and there was a boy in the room, doing something to some herbs at the worktable and humming huskily. Someone had leaned some willow branches in the corner, and they gave off a pleasant, faintly green smell.

He groaned, and immediately the boy brought over a cup, and helped him to drink. The liquid was cool, but horribly bitter.

'I'm Pip,' the boy said, though Cedric couldn't have cared less. 'How are you feeling?'

'Awful,' Cedric grunted. 'Go away.'

But the boy didn't go away. He just stood there, looking gormless.

'Well?!' Cedric croaked crossly. 'What are you staring at?'

'Nothing . . .' The boy – Pip – blushed to the roots of his unruly hair, but he still didn't go away. 'Only . . . it's just that Fosse – the boatman who brought you here? – he said you were from the court of the King . . . '

'And?'

'I was just wondering – how is he? – the King, I mean?' Pip blurted out.

'Why – is he a friend of yours?' Cedric scoffed.

'I, um, saw him in Ely. Last year,' Pip mumbled, looking at his shoes. (In fact Pip did a lot more than just *see* the King, but that is another story.)

'That's right, he *was* there,' Cedric said. 'That'd be when the cursed Sir Robert got his hooks into him—' and he made a rude sign.

Pip gulped. 'Sir Robert – he's not – is he . . . bad?' His voice squeaked part way through.

Cedric sniggered, but he didn't try to send the boy away again. He found he was enjoying all the wide-eyed attention. Obviously, the world *he*, a King's man, moved in was far beyond anything a swamp brat like that could even imagine!

'*Sir Robert*' – he almost spat the name – 'is an eldest son. *Sir Robert* has the King sewn up tight. Nobody else can get a word in edgeways. How am I supposed to become essential to young

Arnald if I can't even get close to him?! The tales I could tell you . . . !'

And without absolutely meaning to, Cedric began to do just that. He began to tell Pip about life at court, and all the slights and insults he'd had to endure there. He told him about his dreams and ambitions to be a power at the top, and how hard it was for a younger son to get ahead. (Cedric could have been a very good-looking man indeed, with his fine features and fair hair and blue eyes, if it weren't for the sour expression that came so easily and so often to his face.)

'My older brother Harold doesn't have any trouble being heard,' he whined. 'My brother Harold has all the money he needs – he's invited to the most select parties, where he wears the most fashionable clothes, and makes influential friends. My father thinks he's *wonderful*, just because he was born first. I tell you, it's hopeless being a younger son *anywhere*, and *especially* at court – it doesn't matter how able you are – no one wants to know! But nobody was going to shove me into a monastery, just to get me out of the way, I can tell you *that* for nothing.' (It didn't occur to him that this might be a rather rude thing to say to someone in a monastery . . .)

It was only by borrowing heavily, and then *bribing* heavily that he'd got this job – this extremely dangerous *mission*, more like! – of going round the country with messages of goodwill from the young King to his devoted subjects. (The important ones, anyway, like the barons and the bishops.)

That was the way the job was described in public, anyway. But that wasn't *all*, of course. While handing out letters and compliments, Cedric was *actually* supposed to be finding out just exactly how devoted the King's subjects really were! He was supposed to keep his eyes and ears wide open, catch every disaffected glance, hear every scheming whisper.

But somehow he managed to stop himself before he told the boy about *that*. He was starting to feel bad again, all hot and wobbly-brained, but even so, some remnant of sense cautioned him against revealing any more of his instructions to a mere fen rat.

Not that it matters, he thought to himself woozily. *Not that it . . .*

Suddenly he sat up and grabbed Pip by the wrist, with unexpected strength. 'I have no intention of dying,' he hissed, staring intently into Pip's startled face. 'Not in a filthy backwater like this – *that's not part of the plan.*' A look of confusion crossed his face. 'I . . . thought I . . .'

He collapsed back onto the mattress.

Pip tucked a blanket round him. Then, with a thoughtful expression on his face, he tiptoed away.

Chapter 4

The Infirmary Has

Another Patient

It was Compline, a few days later, and everyone was tired and ready for their beds. As the last benediction faded into silence, there was a general stir towards the door, when, unexpectedly, it opened from outside, and three figures came in, pausing at the doorstep to cross themselves – two huge men, and a girl.

'Forgive me,' the girl said. 'I am the Lady Rane. I would ask for your help.'

The Lady Rane could not have been more than a year older than

Pip, but she was easily a head taller, and her way of standing, like a spear, made her seem taller still. Though stained with travel, her dress was of a fine-quality linen, and in the light of the candles, her hair glinted like rich exotic gold. The men with her were a matched pair, all muscle and menace and unruly yellow hair. They towered over her, and everyone else in the room besides, but in spite of their threatening presence, it was the Lady who drew the eye. She couldn't have broken you in two with her bare hands, the way they so obviously could, but then, she didn't need to. There was no question of who was in charge.

'My kinsman is sick,' she said, pointing back out into the night. 'I ask you to tend to him, in the name of the saints.'

She spoke with an accent the Brothers would have recognized if they'd spent more time in the market at Ely. But for a moment, it was as if they hadn't understood what she'd said. They just stared. In the continuing silence, she became aware that her veil had fallen down around her shoulders. With a graceful gesture she pulled it back up again, covering the gold of her hair, as was proper in a church. Someone sighed, and with a rustle the Brothers came back to life.

Abbot Michael stepped forward. 'Of course, my child, you and your men are most welcome. Brother Gilbert here is our Infirmarer, but . . .' he frowned a little, then continued, 'I am sorry to say, we have no Guest Hall— ' But she was already shaking her head.

'It is only my kinsman who requires your hospitality, Father. We have brought our own shelter with us. With your permission, the flat ground by the mooring place . . .?'

'Of course, daughter. Brother Gilbert?'

'Pip, go and lay down another mattress in the Infirmary.' Brother Gilbert turned to the Lady. 'Your men will bring the sick one up from your boat?' At her nod he continued. 'This way, then.' He showed no sign of being in awe of her or her huge henchmen, but then he didn't really notice people who were well all that much.

By the time Pip had another straw-filled mattress laid out on the Infirmary floor, they were bringing the sick stranger through the door. Pip stared, curious to see what their new patient was like.

He was not a small man, though he looked dwarfed in the arms of the blond giant who carried him, and he was old, with corded muscles

33

in his thin arms, long wispy white hair and only a weathered scar where his left eye used to be.

'Pip.'

Brother Gilbert beckoned him over, as he made the old man tidy on the mattress.

'See the signs? Shuddering, sweating – and look, a slight yellowing of the skin. Does your head pain you – what is his name?' He peered at the younger man who was looming stolidly in the doorway.

'He's called Haakon,' he said.

Brother Gilbert nodded. 'Haakon. Does your head hurt, Haakon?'

The old man grunted, and shivered more violently.

Brother Gilbert headed for his worktable. 'Go and tell your mistress her kinsman has the ague, and we will do everything we can to draw it out of him,' he said to the henchman. 'Do you understand?'

The young man nodded, and muttered something in a language Pip didn't recognize. It was pretty clear from the tone, though, that he was not being polite. Then he left.

Pip looked questioningly at Brother Gilbert, but the Infirmarer was already involved with his mortar and herbs so he went over to the old man on the mattress and pulled the blanket more tightly around him.

'Thank you, lad.' The sick man spoke with the same strange accent. He nodded towards the door. 'Don't pay any attention to what *he* said.'

'I didn't understand it,' Pip confessed.

The old man snorted. 'He said, "What a waste of time!"'

Pip was indignant. 'Brother Gilbert is the best Infirmarer in the entire world . . .' he began, but the sick man interrupted.

'No, no – it wasn't your Brother Gilbert he meant,' he said. 'It was me. Stopping here for a sick man, when time is so short . . . Anyway, he and his brother already think I'm a waste of time – past it – as useless as this— ' and he pointed at his empty eye socket. 'They call me a waste, but do you know what I call *them*?'

Pip shook his head.

'The twins from Helheim!'

Pip looked blank.

The old man tutted impatiently. 'It's the home of the dishonoured dead. It's where those two hunks of beef belong.' He gave a twisted smile and then closed his eye with a weary sigh.

Just then, Brother Gilbert called Pip over to help with the old man's medicine, and by the time all the work was done, it was late into the night. When the boy's yawns reached the stage of looking to split his face in half, Brother Gilbert finally noticed, and sent him away to his bed.

When the King's man woke again, it was night – that night or some other, he couldn't tell. He felt weak as a kitten, and oddly content to be so. For the moment, the fever had left him, and he was able to look about him with a clear head.

He was no longer alone in the little infirmary. Another straw mattress had been brought in and an old man lay on it, mumbling in his sleep and shifting uneasily. There was something peculiar about his face . . . It took Cedric a moment to realise the man had only one eye.

He lay watching the stranger in the lantern light, idly wondering what the words were that he was trying to say. Something about them was familiar . . . Norse! That was it – he was speaking Norse. Cedric had a smattering of a number of languages – enough anyway to recognize the sounds of them.

Then, for no apparent reason, the man abruptly switched into English.

'Gold,' he said, quite distinctly. 'The Hoard is what we need. We have to find it, before it's too late. It's the only way.'

Then, just as suddenly, he stopped. Cedric held his breath, desperate to hear more. *Gold? What gold?* **Where?!**

But the old man only heaved a great breath, and rolled over onto his side. The rhythmic sound of his snores did nothing to calm Cedric's pulse.

There's more than one way to skin a rabbit, he thought to himself gleefully. *Gold! A Hoard of Gold! And all for me!* It didn't occur to him that the stranger might have just been babbling feverish nonsense, or that, if there *was* gold out there somewhere, he might not want *Cedric* to have it. *He* knew an opportunity *meant for him* when he heard one!

And for the rest of the night, Cedric stared hot-eyed at the ceiling, fantasizing about how much more the King would value him if he were to return . . . *rich*!

Chapter 5

Disturbances

Prior Benet *always* found plenty to complain about when the Brothers met for Chapter (the daily business meeting for the monks) – but over the next few days, there were more things even than usual! And all his discontent centred on one thing: their Norse visitors.

'. . . And another thing – she *said* they were on a trading trip to Ely – she *said* that – but then how did they end up *here*?! *We're* not on the way to Ely!'

'It would seem they lost their way,' said Abbot Michael mildly.

The Prior made a sound that, coming from any other man, in any other setting, would have been a rather common snort.

Abbot Michael sighed. 'Is there something specific you wish to complain of, my son?'

But that was the problem – there wasn't anything *specific*.

The old man was too ill to do more than shiver and sweat. The twins from Helheim – their names were Leif and Olaf – swaggered quite a lot, but they weren't doing anything actually *wrong*. With the Abbot's permission, they'd set up camp on the bit of flat ground by the shore. (In winter it would have been much too soggy, but the hot summer sun had dried the ground weeks ago.) They'd pitched a tent for the Lady, with fine carved beasts' heads on the crosspieces. Certainly the wool cloth it was covered with had yellowed, and someone had darned it in a number of places. But you could hardly complain in Chapter about *that*.

Which only left the Lady herself. At no point had anyone seen her behaving in any way unseemly, and yet, she was . . . disturbing. And it wasn't only because she was a young female. The monastery was part of the Fen community, not shut off from it, and she was not the first pretty girl to come to Wickit. It was something else. The Lady Rane was *different* – exotic, unlikely, a breath of fresh air, wild like the open sea . . . *golden*. In their minds, the Brothers looked for the right words, and often found, instead, memories of things long forgotten, from childhood, or stories of far-away places that had stirred them once, emotions and dreams from the time before the habit of Wickit became so wholly familiar. It was as if the roving Viking blood that ran through her veins stirred up echoes in their own.

Even the Abbot was affected.

When Pip turned up for his Latin lesson later that morning, he found the Lady Rane there before him, and Abbot Michael looking unusually pink-faced and bright-eyed. Pip stared at him, his eyebrows disappearing under his shaggy mop of hair.

'We've been talking about mountains,' the Abbot said, with a longing note in his voice Pip had never heard before. 'I remember so well how it was for me, at first . . . how all this flatness can make you feel. When it's mountains you're used to. It's as if it were only yesterday . . .'

There was a pause, in which Pip was overwhelmed by a quite ridiculous jealousy of everybody in the whole world who'd ever seen a mountain, and Lady Rane and the Abbot in particular. Then, 'How *does* it make you feel?' he asked, in spite of himself.

'As if you're about to fall up into the sky,' Rane answered the question, not looking at him but down at her hands, clenched in her lap.

Abbot Michael reached across and patted her shoulder.

'It passes, though, my child. You can be sure of that. There's nothing we can't get used to, with God's help.'

She looked up then, and the smile on her face and the way her eyes crinkled at the corners made Pip's heart turn over.

God's Eyebrows! he thought.

Definitely unsettling.

The Latin lesson had been awful – Abbot Michael really didn't seem to be concentrating – and Pip was glad when it was over. At least the next job he had wasn't going to be upsetting anyone.

Or so he thought.

He went first to the kitchen, and then into the church to collect the Wickit silver. Perfect dropped down out of the eaves and slid into his hood to keep him company. He laid his work out in the doorway of the church to catch the good light, and set to, polishing away with Brother Barnard's special cleaning concoction and a lot of elbow grease. Pip didn't mind this job. The cross that stood on the altar, the best candlesticks, the chalice and plate for the Mass – they were all beautiful. He'd spent many an hour keeping them untarnished and glittering. They were like old friends. Pip started to feel better. More at ease . . .

But he was being watched. He was in clear view of the camp by the shore, and though the Lady Rane was nowhere about, the twins from Helheim *were*. The sight of all that silver excited very different emotions in *them* – emotions that would have justified Prior Benet in every bad thought he'd ever had about them, if only he'd known!

The Prior would have guessed immediately that something dodgy was up when Leif and Olaf approached the Lady Rane that evening by her tent. It was obvious they had something to say, and also obvious they were more than a bit nervous about saying it. They kept shoving each other forward and then whispering furiously together. It would have been funny if it hadn't been so irritating.

It certainly didn't take long for Rane's patience to run out.

'Well?' she said, tapping her foot.

'It's just . . .'

'We thought . . .'

More shuffling and scuffing of shoes.

'WHAT did you think?!' snapped Rane. 'You, Olaf, *you* tell me. *Now.*'

'Well, Lady, it's just that . . . today we saw the boy cleaning the things – the church things – and they're as valuable as any Hoard—'

'And they're right *here*, to hand – no more looking – we could go *home*—'

'Everything we need, right here! And you know our time is running out. We really should be getting back, with the summer nearly over—'

' – and your father only half a man—'

With an utterly unexpected speed and viciousness, Rane hit Olaf in the face with all her strength, leaving a reddening mark behind. Leif was quicker by a sliver, and got out of reach just in time.

'Your lord, my father, is *sick*,' she said in a tight, cold voice. 'He will get *better*. And when he *is* better, *I* do not choose to be the one to tell him his people behaved like common thieves the moment they were out from under his eyes.'

There was only the briefest pause before Olaf put his fist up to his chest and bowed. At once, Leif followed his brother's lead.

'We are under *your* eyes, Lady,' he rumbled. 'It shall be as you say.'

Only when she was sure she was alone, did Rane let the look of outraged righteousness on her face fade away. She stared up into the sky and murmured to herself,

'But if the Hoard isn't there . . . it *must* be there – I *know* it's there . . . but if we can't find it . . . *then* it will be time to think of the Wickit silver . . . '

The Prior would have had plenty to say in Chapter if he'd been lucky enough to witness *this* disturbance, but no one saw the scene, beyond the participants. For the next few days, the twins swaggered a bit less and sulked a lot more. And the Lady Rane waited, and watched.

Another hot day dawned, and Cedric the King's man (on Brother Gilbert's orders) tottered out of the Infirmary to sit in the sun and gather his strength again. For a while he was content to do just that. But then, he noticed the boy. It was the one who worked in the Infirmary and kept bringing him that awful medicine. He was doing some sort of work down by the shore today.

Then he noticed the boy was watching something, though trying to look as if he wasn't. Then he saw what it was that had caught the lad's attention.

It was the Norse girl. She was sitting at the entrance to her tent, braiding her golden hair.

It was a pretty sight, but Cedric spared it no more than a glance. It was what he could see *behind* the girl that interested *him*. The front flaps of the tent had been looped back to let in a little air. From where he was sitting, Cedric could see everything the shelter contained – and it wasn't very much. A pile of ferns that was the Lady's bed. A few spare clothes, neatly folded. And, right at the back of the tent, one extremely interesting-looking wooden box.

46

Cedric licked his lips, and smiled to himself.

Cedric was not the only one to be intrigued by that box.

Prior Benet had set Pip to cleaning the wax from the flagstones of the church. With so many people about it wasn't safe for Perfect to do it for him, (she had her own technique which involved carefully controlled flaming and then licking the softened wax up with her tongue) so he was reduced to the old way of scrabble and scrape. When Brother Barnard stuck his head through the door and called for his help, Pip was delighted. He got up off his knees and rushed after the Cellarer – he was sure *any* job would be an improvement! That is, until he realised it was *eel-gutting* Brother Barnard wanted him for . . .

The Cellarer didn't stop laughing for ages after he saw Pip's face. Then, when that palled, he decided to pass the time by having a go at guessing what their Norse visitors had in that mysterious box.

'It'll be something *very* precious,' he stated emphatically.

Pip was trying not to breathe in – some of the eels had been around for a while, and their insides weren't exactly sweet smelling. They were bound for the smokehouse, and for salting. 'Why?' he grunted.

'Use your brain, boy!' Brother Barnard bellowed cheerfully. 'All the way across the wide, wild sea and only *one box* to make it worth while?! Of *course* they've got something precious in there! But what . . .?'

Pepper from the East was Brother Barnard's favourite guess, with ginger root running a close second.

'Or maybe, cubeb . . .' (Pepper would have travelled all the way from India, but the cubeb peppercorns came from even further afield.)

Pip found that all the speculation about exotic, aromatic spices helped him with ignoring the very un-exotic smell of eel guts.

Brother Gilbert came by, and was drawn into the conversation too.

'There was a time when I thought I might go to those places myself,' he said in a soft voice. 'There is so much to learn of medicine from the East.'

'I heard tell that cinnamon grows not far

48

from the Garden of Paradise,' said Brother Barnard, not really listening to him. 'And cardamom. They sometimes call it "Grains of Paradise", did you know that? What a flavour!'

'Fields of saffron stretching out as far as the eye can see. It would be something to be able to say, "I was there. I saw that."'

There was a long thoughtful pause. Then the two men sighed.

'I'll finish here, lad,' said Brother Barnard, suddenly sounding unusually subdued. 'Go clean yourself up, and head back to the Infirmary. Assuming you want him?' This to Brother Gilbert.

The Infirmarer nodded absent-mindedly, and Pip made his escape, happy to leave the gloomy mood behind along with the stink.

By the time Pip managed to scrub himself reasonable-smelling again, it was almost time for Vespers. Brother Gilbert was looking out for him from the door of the Infirmary.

'Pip, there you are. Go and find her,' he called. He didn't have to say who the 'her' was.

Pip ran, not waiting to hear if the news was good or bad. He found the Lady Rane by the shore, staring off into the distance.

'Brother Gilbert asks you to come right away, Lady,' he panted. She gave him a single stricken look, and ran.

'He's asking for you, girl!' Brother Gilbert didn't care much about rank when he was working. 'In with you, now – hurry up!'

Rane rushed headlong into the cool dimness of the Infirmary. Pip followed – and saw  her skid to a stop and drop to her knees by Haakon's pallet with a cry of pleasure. The old man was sitting up, looking wrung out and frail, but with his one eye clear and bright, and a welcoming smile on his face.

'My kinsman – is it possible?!' she exclaimed, in Norse. 'Are you well?!'

'Speak English, my Lady, in courtesy to our hosts. And to show we have nothing to hide.' The old man 's voice quavered with weakness, but the girl took the reprimand with a grave nod.

'And yes, it is possible,' he continued. 'The good Brother tells me the worst is past.'

The girl gave a smothered gasp and grabbed the sick man's hand in both of hers. He gave her a weary smile.

'It is good to see you, my Lady,' he said. 'But now I must sleep again.'

'Of course.' She sounded a bit watery, but rose to her feet. She turned to leave, but then he spoke again.

'Thank you,' he rumbled softly. 'With time so short, you shouldn't have waited for me, but . . . you have my gratitude.'

The girl nodded solemnly, and went out.

There was a bench just outside the door. The Lady Rane suddenly flopped down on it as if her knees had given out on her. She dragged in a great gulp of air, and then let it go again in a long whoosh.

'My Lady?' Pip had followed her, uncertain what else he should be doing. 'Are you all right?'

'I couldn't believe it when he fell ill,' she said, and there was a wobble in her voice. 'It was like my father all over again, I thought. But your Brother Gilbert is a saint' – she turned to Pip with a radiant smile – 'and he brought him back to me.'

All of a sudden, she didn't look like a lady any more. She just looked like . . . a person.

Somebody who'd been tight as a cramp with worry for far too long and who'd found a moment of unexpected ease.

Just then, the bell began to ring.

'Shouldn't you be going to service?' she asked, sitting up straighter.

Pip shook his head. 'I think Brother Gilbert will want someone to stay close to your kinsman. In case he needs anything in the next while.'

She gave a slight nod, and then patted the bench beside her. 'I'm glad he's in such good hands. But sit now. I'm sure you're tired, and you'll be able to hear him perfectly well from here.'

As Pip hesitated, Brother Gilbert came out of the Infirmary.

'Stay put, and keep your ears open, boy,' he said. 'The old man should sleep soundly for a good while now, but I'll be back after Vespers to check on him.'

He hurried off as the bell died away. Rane patted the bench again, and Pip, not knowing how to get out of it, sat down. He felt Perfect shuffle round in his hood so he could lean back more comfortably if he wanted to, but he was much too tense for that.

It was very quiet for a moment, and then, Rane spoke. 'You know you're dying to ask me questions. Why don't you just get on with it?' she said. 'I don't mind.'

Pip nearly fell off the bench, but she seemed to mean it.

'Well,' he said. 'I did wonder . . . how do you all know so many languages?'

The girl shrugged. 'You can't trade if you can't talk,' she said. 'Anyway, my mother was English.' She gave him a small, almost shy smile. 'My father over-wintered in Jorvik – you call it York – one year, and brought her home with him in the spring. He always said it was the best trading season he ever had.' The smile faded.

Pip suddenly realised he desperately didn't want her to start looking sad again, so he asked the next thing that popped into his head.

'What's in the box?' he squeaked, and then wondered if he'd overstepped the line.

The expression on her face was hard to read. She didn't *seem* offended.

'The Brothers have been trying to guess,' Pip blundered on. 'Brother Barnard, of course, thinks in terms of kitchen things, and he was wondering if it was full of pepper. Or maybe cinnamon. And

Brother Gilbert thinks all the strange and wonderful medicines of the East could be in it, from all the places he's never been . . .' He trailed off.

Rane kept very still for a moment. 'Those are good guesses,' she said in a neutral sort of voice, 'but they're all wrong. Shall I tell you what that box is *really* full of?' She was watching him intently now.

Pip gulped, and nodded.

Rane leaned closer and whispered in his ear.

'It's full of nothing. It's empty.'

Pip pulled away from her and stared. What kind of person went trading with nothing to sell? Unless . . .

'You're not here for trading, are you,' he said, and it wasn't a question. He could feel Perfect stirring in his hood. She was as tense as he was.

Rane looked at him for a long moment with those cool blue eyes. This time, though he felt the colour flood his face, he didn't look away.

'You're right,' she answered at last. 'I'm not here to trade. I'm here for something much more important . . .'

Rane's Tale

'I am a direct descendant of Johan Shortleg,' she began, then paused dramatically.

She obviously expected some sort of reaction, but Pip had never heard the name before.

'Um, his name was Shortleg?' he asked. 'But . . . why?'

Rane looked irritated. 'Because he had one leg shorter than the other!' she said abruptly. 'He broke it when he was a boy and the bone never set the way it should.'

'Ah, yes.' Pip nodded solemnly, feeling he was on familiar ground here. 'Brother Gilbert has explained this to me. It's a question of the correct tension when splinting . . . Er, you were telling me about your ancestor?'

Rane sighed, and continued with her story. 'I'm sure I don't need to tell you that Johan Short-leg was one of the last, and one of the greatest Viking raiders that ever lived.'

Pip tried to look as if he had *really* known that, but had just forgotten for a moment.

'Like other Vikings before him, Johan came to raid, and then stayed on, to settle and trade. He spent a good number of years *here*, in your Fenland. But after a time his men began to long for the sight of mountains again, and eventually Johan agreed to pack up his plunder and go. It was the last he was to see of this place, for he fell ill on the voyage home and died not long after they arrived. He probably picked up some disease from his time here . . . '

Pip tried not to take offence at the way she wrinkled up her nose as she looked about.

'The story of his exploits and his tragically ignoble death – the life of a hero-warrior, and the death of a coward – all that has been told and told again. But what *isn't* told is the fact that he actually meant to *come back* to the Fens someday

– that he didn't bring *all* his goods away with him. He left some of his great wealth behind, here in the marshland, safely buried in a place that only he could find.' Her own voice had dropped to a husky whisper.

Pip's eyes went wide. He'd heard stories about Viking Hoards – fabulous wealth hidden in the marshes that no one could find, guarded by heathen ghosts and terrible curses . . . 'You mean, he left buried treasure – and died without telling anybody where?!' he croaked.

Rane leaned closer. 'Oh, but he *did* tell!' she said. 'Apparently, on his deathbed, almost with his last breath, Johan had a slave write down directions to his Hoard, and then told him to hide the manuscript away among Johan's things. He presumably had the slave killed then. And the manuscript wasn't found. It was forgotten – it just dropped out of sight for years and years, until even the slightest rumour of its existence died away. It was as if no one was supposed to find it until it was *needed.'*

'Why do you think that?' asked Pip, his eyes round.

'Because I *did* find the manuscript – at a

57

time when our need for it could not have been more sore.'

'You found it?! Where?'

'At the bottom of the meanest-looking chest, at the back of a storeroom used only for rubbish and broken things beyond repair . . . I was looking in the last place I could think of for something – *anything* – that we could sell. Anything that could bring us back from the edge of ruin . . .'

And she began to tell him the story of that ruin. As he listened, Pip was astonished that so many disastrous things could happen to just one family. It was as if all the bad luck in the world had been drawn to that single fjord. Their crops withered in the fields. Their fishing boats sank in storms. Their trading expeditions came back unsuccessful – or didn't come back at all. The staggers took their cattle and sheep. Rane's brothers and kinsmen (there seemed to be scores of them – Pip couldn't keep track) were lost in one accident or catastrophe after another, until finally there was only Rane and her father left, trying to hold everything together.

'The serfs think we are cursed,' she said in a low voice. 'They're sure my family has offended Loki somehow, and he is exacting his revenge on us.'

Pip was puzzled. 'Loki?' he said.

'They're just serfs,' Rane said with a shrug. 'Little better than . . . well, what can you expect.'

'Um . . . so, your father sent you here?' Pip asked hesitantly.

'No!' She shook her head so hard her braids flapped. 'I came of my own choice. I didn't show him the manuscript – he never would have given his permission for me to come. He would have insisted on coming himself, but since his illness . . .'

'This illness – did you know what it was?'

'Apoplexy,' she replied. 'He fell down all of a sudden, right in front of me, and then his right hand wouldn't move, and his words were muddled—' Rane looked as if she were seeing it happen all over again. Then she turned on Pip so fiercely it made him gulp. 'But *he was getting better, I swear, or I never would have left!*'

'I believe you,' he yelped. Then, more quietly, 'I believe you. Finish your story.'

There was not much more to tell. What pushed Rane into the fateful search in the storeroom, and then her mad treasure hunt over the sea, was a proposal of marriage. The man to whom they were so deeply in debt came to them and offered to make Rane his wife, in exchange for all the money the family owed.

'He said he would have *me* as his betrothed, or everything else,' she said. Her voice sounded wooden. 'We had till the end of the summer to decide which it was to be.'

Their time is *running out!* Pip thought.

'And you didn't . . . like this man, then?' he asked tentatively. Rane might be too young to marry, but she was not too young to be promised.

'I . . . to be honest, he seemed an unobjectionable sort of man, not too old, pleasant enough. Under other circumstances, I might consider him favourably . . . but to promise to go to him as things stood – I'd be no better than a debt-thrall! *It would be dishonourable.* That was when I realised I had to come here, and recover my ancestor's gold. Don't you see?! With Johan's Hoard, I wouldn't *need* to marry like that. I'd have more than enough to pay our debts, set us up with some new boats, make an appeasement offering to Loki – to satisfy the serfs. And something for the church, as well. Of course. You can *see* it was the only way.'

Pip knew she expected an answer, but he was too overwhelmed by her story just then to respond properly. It was all so . . . *big*, compared to his life. Disasters, ancient family secrets, buried treasure – it made being an under-sized orphan boy in a tiny fen abbey seem like nothing . . .

. . . and yet, she'd chosen him to tell her story to.

*Why **was** that?* he asked himself, belatedly.

Rane had been watching him intently. She looked at lot like a cat watching a mouse.

'But what about *your* story, Pip?' she said softly, looking into his eyes in a disconcerting way. 'I've told you so much – isn't there something *you'd* like to tell *me?*'

Pip gulped and shook his head. He tried to edge away but she had him backed into a corner . . .

'I think there is, though, Pip,' she went on. 'I think that, even though I've told you everything, you are keeping something back from me.' Her pale blue eyes hypnotised him so that he could barely breathe. 'In *fact*—'

Her hand shot past Pip's ear fast as a striking snake, and before he could even cry out, she'd dragged Perfect out of his hood by her tail and held her, upside down in plain view.

'In fact,' the Lady Rane stated triumphantly, 'I *know* it!'

Chapter 7

*F*lying Dragons?

'How did you find out?!' Pip asked as soon as he could breathe again. 'We've always been so careful!'

Rane had made a proper apology to Perfect for her disrespectful treatment, and the dragon was safely out of sight again in Pip's hood. Only her little worried face showed from under his left ear. Both boy and gargoyle were thoroughly shocked at the way Rane had found out their secret. No one Perfect hadn't deliberately shown herself to had ever known of her existence before. Any unplanned glimpses Pip had always managed to explain away. It was a rat they'd seen, or a bat or a passing bird or a trick of the light – almost *anything* other than the truth. But Rane had gone straight for Perfect's favourite hiding place as if it had a big sign over it saying, 'Hey Look There's a Gargoyle in Here!'

'So, I was right,' murmured Rane. 'Not everybody knows about her.'

'*No one* knows about her!' Pip snapped.

'Except . . .' Perfect began, but Pip shook his head sharply. He wasn't bringing the King into this. That was none of Rane's business. *Perfect* was none of her business. *None* of it was anything to *do* with her—

He hated how calm the Norse girl looked. As if she hadn't just turned his world upside down.

'We have ones like her,' she was saying. 'Of wood, though. Not stone. I've never seen one close up, for our churches are much taller than your Wickit church, and the flying dragons are only on the highest parts of the roof.'

'You've seen dragons?! Flying?!' Pip's heart leapt.

But she shook her head. 'No, I just meant they are carved *as if* they are flying. Our wood carvers are among the most skilful in all the world.'

'My Maker was *the* most skilful *stone*-carver

in the world – *ever!*' Perfect protested shrilly.

Rane raised a hand. 'I think there can be no doubt about that,' she said, sounding almost humble.

Perfect subsided, but Pip could feel the way the tip of her tail was still twitching about agitatedly.

'I think I spotted you because of them, though,' Rane continued thoughtfully. 'The wooden dragons, I mean. Of course, in my country we are not quite so quick to think everything strange and wonderful comes from the Devil. And' – she shrugged – 'it could also be because I've had nothing else to do, these last days, *except* wait and watch.'

Then, in what seemed to Pip like a complete change of subject, she said, 'I'm convinced now, that it really is practically impossible for anyone who doesn't know the Fens to follow Johan's instructions. Even *without* taking into account how things change here. He wrote in riddles and clues that would have made sense to him, fresh from years in this land, but for us . . . ! So this is what I want to say . . .'

But, whatever it was, she didn't get a chance to say it. Out of nowhere, they were being loomed at by a furious Prior Benet, his habit flapping with the speed of his arrival, and his finger wagging aggressively in Pip's face.

'Did you *hear* the bell for service?' he hissed.

'Yes, but—'

'Did you *attend* the service?'

'No, but—'

'Have you even finished cleaning the church?'

'No, but—'

'Can you think of any reason why I should not immediately report you to the Abbot?' The Prior's voice rose practically to a shriek.

Pip hung his head. He knew there was nothing he could do – the Prior had been out to get someone for days. It had only been a matter of time before that someone turned out to be *him*. It was a storm he'd just have to weather. No point in talking back. It would only make things worse – much, much worse . . .

But Rane didn't see it that way.

'I can offer a number of reasons,' she said coolly. 'One would be because he hasn't done anything wrong. Two would be because he's been doing what your Infirmarer told him to do, which was not go to the service, but instead to remain here, in case my kinsman or the other ill man had need of him. And a third reason would be that I haven't finished with him yet.'

Pip, Perfect and Prior Benet all stopped breathing. The tiny bit of Pip's brain which had not shut down watched in fascinated horror as the Prior's face went first deathly white, and then an apoplectic purple.

'You haven't heard the last of this,' he hissed through clenched teeth, and Pip knew that whatever trouble he'd been in before, it had just doubled.

As the Prior stormed off, Rane tutted disapprovingly.

'He's very rude, isn't he,' she said calmly. 'In my country, the monks show more respect. I will talk to you later.' And with that, she stood up, shook out her skirts and walked away, leaving Pip gaping like a beached fish behind her.

He spent the rest of the day waiting for the sky to fall, but, in spite of some looks of pure loathing from Prior Benet, Pip managed to get through to bedtime in one piece.

'What a day!' he sighed to Perfect as he flopped gratefully onto his pallet in the darkness of the kitchen.

Perfect gave a whimper of agreement and then opened her small mouth in a huge yawn.

'At least we don't have to worry about anything else until tomorrow,' she said.

She could not have been more wrong.

'Pip? Where are you? I want to talk to you!' The voice from the doorway was Rane's. It was soft enough, but much too urgent for comfort.

'Go away!' Pip whispered back, trying to disappear under his bed cover. 'I'm not here! I don't want to talk to you – I'm in enough trouble as it is!'

The Lady Rane's tut was becoming altogether too familiar.

'I *am* going away,' she said. 'Right now, tonight. But not until I've talked to you.'

Pip groaned. Rane continued relentlessly.

'You know what I said to you before,' she said. 'How only a local person would be able to read Johan's directions after all these years, understand his clues and riddles, especially with the way the fens shift and change? Well, I've decided you're the one. You're the local person I need . . .' Her voice changed. 'I can't believe you could really want to *stay* in this horrible little place, Pip,' she said, 'so don't pretend! I know I can't find the Hoard without help, and you're the one who's going to give me that help. I've told you the whole story, and I know I can count on you to keep my secret.'

'*How* do you know?' Pip blustered despairingly. 'What makes you think I won't just go and tell Abbot Michael or Prior Benet or anybody all about your buried treasure?'

Her eyes glittered in the dim light from the doorway.

'Because,' she said softly, 'if you tell my secret, you know that I'll tell yours.'

There was a moment so silent Pip could hear her breathing.

'You wouldn't!' he said.

'I would,' said Rane.

'Oh, dear,' whispered Perfect. 'And she would at that.'

He saw Rane come into the room and straight towards him.

'Give me your hand,' she ordered, and Pip found himself doing as he was told. He reached out his hand in the darkness and the girl took it between her two cool ones in an oddly formal gesture.

'This is my oath to you,' she said solemnly. 'If you will help me to come safely to my ancestor's treasure and go safely with it back to my ship, so that I may return to my country with my freedom and my honour still my own, then I swear to keep the secret of your dragon to my dying day and beyond. I give you my bond.'

Pip's mind darted about wildly, desperate to find a way out. He didn't want to leave Wickit! He might have wished his life wasn't so boring – but he certainly didn't want to have any part in *this* adventure with these frightening, disturbing people! But if Perfect's existence became known, then the witch-hunters and the exorcists would be all over them in a flash. Even if he'd wanted to, Abbot Michael wouldn't be able to protect them . . .

He looked at Rane pleadingly, but he knew there was no escape. There would be no weakening in the girl who held his hand in hers, no wavering or backing off. She knelt on the floor, calmly waiting for him to do as she expected.

He gulped, and gave in. With a heavy heart,

he dragged his hand away from hers and whispered, 'Yes.'

'You swear?'

'Yes! Yes, I swear. Now go away and let me sleep,' he added under his breath. She didn't seem to hear.

'That's fine. Let's go.'

'**WHAT?!**' Pip squawked, but Rane's voice was as calm as ever.

'We're leaving tonight,' she said. 'We're leaving now.'

Chapter 8

Riddles and Runes

'The next part of the manuscript uses the stars to guide us – and I'm not waiting another whole day in this place! Now that my kinsman is out of danger I can spare no more time,' Rane continued. 'The summer is drawing to a close – the sea crossing can take many days if the weather or the winds are unkind – and the colder days start sooner in my land than they do here. Our debtor won't wait beyond the first frost.'

'B-but . . .' stammered Pip. 'You're going to leave Haakon *behind* . . .?!'

She nodded impatiently. 'He is too weak to come with us, but he will get better now. Before very long, he will be well enough to travel! I can go now with a clear heart, find my ancestor's treasure, and then come back for him. By then, God willing, he will be strong enough to come back with us to our ship – and then for home!' Her smile blazed.

'But first, I will take my leave of him,' she said, visibly reining herself in. 'So that he knows what I am about, and that I will be coming again to retrieve him. Olaf and Leif are already preparing the boat. Come on!'

Sooner than he would have thought possible, Pip found himself sitting in the Norse punt, with Perfect huddled silently in his hood, and the island of Wickit disappearing behind them in the darkness. He'd gone with Rane to the Infirmary and waited by the door, but the conversation between her and Haakon had been in whispers, and he hadn't heard much of what they'd said. The old man argued, but only a little – he seemed to see it was the best plan. At the last moment, Pip tried to persuade him to tell Abbot Michael or Brother Gilbert what was going on – why Pip wasn't going to be there in the morning! – but without success. Haakon just shook his head, shut his one eye and turned away.

As soon as they had pushed off from the shore and were out of earshot of the monastery, Rane gave her orders.

'There are two sets of directions,' she told them, 'one using the winter sky and one for now, for the summer. *"Take the Pole Star for your shoulder bird and fix your eyes on the stars of the Great Dog for as long as it takes a strong man to walk from the hall of my family to the best bog iron seam and back again."'*

The twins appeared to be calculating the distance – which no one from outside Rane's family's fjord could have! – and nodded. Leif took up the pole while Rane balanced herself in the prow. She checked the sky over her left shoulder, then looked ahead, and pointed.

'That way,' she said.

Leif adjusted the punt to match her direction, and dug in the pole.

And that was that. Now Pip was out in the Fens in the dead of night, his lot bound to people he hadn't even known existed a month ago. He felt awful.

They travelled in silence for what seemed like hours until, at last, Olaf spoke.

'Almost there, Lady,' he grunted. He had taken over the punting from his brother some time ago.

Rane nodded, and turned.

'Pip,' she said. 'I need to show you something.'

The boat lurched slightly as she made her way back to him. She huddled down and, using her cloak to shield it, lit a horn-lantern. The gold glow lit up her face and at the same time drew the dark wings of the night in around them, so that it felt to Pip as if they were the only people in the whole world.

She pulled a roll of vellum out of her pouch and spread it out reverently across her knees.

'Here it is,' she said. 'Johan Shortleg's manuscript.'

Pip craned forward, curious in spite of himself, but then leaned back again almost at once.

'I can't read that!' he said.

'No, I wouldn't have thought you could. It's in runes.' She traced a line of markings at the top of the page. 'These first ones, here, gave us a latitude for the landing place, and an inlet where we could leave the longboat and a few crew without drawing too much attention to them. That was straightforward enough but, unfortunately, the instructions are not all so easy. I think my ancestor fancied himself a bit of a skald.'

'A bit of a . . .?'

'It means "bard". He wrote some of his instructions in the form of riddles or little poems. This part, for example. It took me a while to understand what he meant by *"The houses of the men of skirts"* but there was a star reference we could use to get started, and then, when Haakon became ill and I knew a monastery was what I *needed*, it suddenly clicked in my mind that that was where Johan was sending me *anyway*!'

Pip made a choking noise. 'You mean, Wickit was just part of your treasure hunt?!'

'How else do you think we would have found you?' Rane looked surprised. 'Your monastery is very small, Pip, and the Fenland is large. *Very* large. But look here. When we finish this stage of the journey, the next instruction, here' – and she pointed to some markings – 'isn't anything obvious like a star reference or a latitude. All it says is *"Find and follow the straight road*". Another riddle.' She looked at him expectantly. 'What does it mean?'

'Are you sure you've read it right?' said Pip, frowning. 'You don't *get* roads in the Fenland – it's too soft. There are paths over bits of it, yes, but they don't just go in a straight line from here to there. They have to follow the firm ground, and that can be all over the place.' He made a wavy line with his hand.

'But if it's a riddle,' Rane said, 'he wouldn't be meaning a real road. Think, Pip – what else could he be talking about? Something that's straight . . .'

Pip shook his head. 'This is crazy! Why didn't he just say what he meant? I have no idea what he could *possibly* be going on abou . . .' His voice trailed off. 'Unless . . .' He looked at her uncertainly. 'Unless he meant . . . the old Roman drainage canal?'

Rane laughed out loud. 'The rascal – of course that's what he meant. They always built straight, the Romans, didn't they, and water is the road round here!' She was delighted with the answer. 'Right, how do we get there? Can you show us the way?' Her eyes sparkled with excitement in the lantern light.

'Well, yes,' Pip spluttered, 'but that's *hours* away! And it's practically morning *already*!'

'We'll sleep later.' Rane stood up carefully. 'Just tell Olaf which channel to take.'

'I can't see why we should do all the work around here,' rumbled Olaf sulkily. 'Let the boy take his turn, if he's the one who knows the way.'

'Fine,' said Rane, settling herself more comfortably on the floor of the punt. 'Carry on.'

Pip sighed, and stood up. The others left him to it.

He knew the channels this near Wickit like his own skin, and as he poled along there was nothing to distract him from his troubles. He looked up into the star-speckled sky and thought about home. Everyone would be fast asleep there. No one would even know he was gone, not until Brother Barnard came in from Prime to make breakfast. If only he'd been able to convince the old Norseman to explain to Abbot Michael . . . What would they all be thinking of him!

A coward. A no-good run-away. An ungrateful dog. Prior Benet would be saying, 'I told you so!' from dawn to dusk, and no one would be able to disagree.

But he'd given his word. He couldn't get around it, or over it, or out of it. The only thing he could do, was do it.

And then it struck him – it wasn't just his reputation that was in danger. As long as these people needed him, he was safe enough, but what about *afterwards*? Suppose he helped them all the way to the buried treasure, what was to stop them slitting his throat as soon as his usefulness was over? Olaf and Leif would be perfectly willing to do it, he was certain, and he wasn't *absolutely* sure that Rane would get in their way. He had no clear idea what *her* limits were, where *she* drew the line . . .

One horrible thought led to another.

If the Lady Rane had it in mind to steal Perfect, the best way to do that would be to kill Pip.

He felt the gargoyle stir unhappily in his hood. And so, partly to reassure her that, in spite of the evidence, all would be well, and partly to reassure himself, Pip began to hum.

Chapter 9

*H*aakon's Dream

Back at the Infirmary, Haakon was tired. He'd been very ill, and he was not a young man, and he was asleep again almost before Rane and Pip left. And as he slept, he had a dream. He dreamed that the English man on the other pallet stood up, collected his things and, moving silently, stealthily, with many anxious glances over at Haakon, he crept out into the darkness of the night.

What an odd thing to dream! Haakon thought to himself. *I wonder where he's going? I wonder what it signifies?*

Which was when he woke up. In a flash, the old man realised that the dream was no dream.

81

Cedric really *was* gone, and Haakon knew *exactly* what it signified!

Chapter 10

Where Are They?

What makes a doctor wake in the middle of the night and feel compelled to go and check on Patient X? Whatever that instinct is, it woke Brother Gilbert out of a wonderfully sound sleep, and impelled him to pad off to his Infirmary in the cool darkness. Once there, he felt for the lantern just inside the door and lit it, being careful to shield any glare, so as not disturb the sleepers in the room.

He needn't have bothered, for when he turned round, he realised there was no one there. Both his patients had disappeared! For a moment he just stood, his kind, ugly face a picture of astonishment.

There was no sign of Cedric or the old Norseman. Just their empty mattresses, the blankets tumbled onto the floor.

Brother Gilbert scratched at his tonsure, trying to think clearly. They were such an unlikely pair – what in heaven's name could they be *doing* together!

He trotted over to the kitchen to consult his assistant.

'Pip?' he called softly from the door. 'Wake up! The strangest thing has happened – they've both disappeared! The King's man and the Norse. Come and help me look for them. Pip? *Pip*?!' He opened the lantern door and took a proper look into the kitchen.

Which was when Brother Gilbert realised it was not just his *patients* who were gone . . .

Moving steadily, purposefully, he searched the island from one end to the other . . . there was no sign of Pip, Cedric, Rane, or the two heavies anywhere in Wickit. The Norse boat was missing, and *both* the monastery punts as well.

Without any further delay, Brother Gilbert went to his Abbot.

' . . . they were better, Father, both men, but not what you'd call *well* . . . And the boy – he's never done anything like this before. Never.'

'Was there any sign of a struggle? Could they all have been, what, kidnapped?' Abbot Michael asked.

Brother Gilbert could only shake his head. 'No, Father. No sign of anything like that. They all just . . . left!' Then it suddenly seemed to occur to him that he'd dragged his Abbot out of bed in the middle of the night. 'I ... I'm sorry, Father, perhaps I should have waited to speak with you . . .?'

'No, no, of course not,' Abbot Michael reassured him. 'You did right to bring this matter to me at once. Leave it with me now. I will pray a while, and think what is best to do.' Then, as the Infirmarer turned to go, he added, 'And Brother, you pray too, yes?'

Brother Gilbert arrived at Chapter next morning in an unaccustomed turmoil. With anything medical, he usually knew where he was – but this was a mystery no herb or decoction could help with. Perhaps he *should* have waited longer before reporting the absences – especially Pip's! – to the Abbot. Perhaps there was some explanation he'd missed, and he'd dropped the boy into a pot of trouble for no need. Perhaps he should have kept it all hushed-up and hidden for as long as possible . . .

Not much chance of that with Prior Benet about! His was the first voice raised.

' . . . so I checked, and the King's man – and the . . . that girl and her men – they're all gone, *and* the Norse boat **and**, would you believe it, both our boats . . .'

'Yes, my son. I know,' said Abbot Michael mildly, but the Prior was still in full flow.

' . . . as I've said from the beginning, if you harbour thieves, you can't be surprised at being robbed. Not that I ever knew anything against the King's man – he *looked* honest enough. But those *others*! And *then* I discovered that the boy was gone as well!'

'Yes,' said Abbot Michael, a little more firmly this time. 'I know.'

'Though, of course, the reason for *that* is obvious. He knew he was going to be punished, so he ran away. The only thing surprising in that is that it didn't happen years ago. *As I have always said —*'

'My son, you are not listening,' said Abbot Michael, and this time his voice was pure steel. 'I am already aware of what you are telling me. Thank you for your . . . vigilance. It has been noted. As to the events of this night, all will be made clear to you in God's good time. I do not intend to speak on these matters again until then.'

He rose and walked out, and the Brothers scurried after him. Prior Benet was left standing, mouth open, a look of bewildered dissatisfaction on his face.

Outside in the sunlight, Brother Gilbert scrubbed an anxious hand over his tonsure. The Abbot hadn't lied – not in so many words – but he *had* implied that it was not only God who had tabs on what had happened. The Infirmarer did not doubt the power of prayer – maybe God *had* spoken to Abbot Michael in the night and explained everything.

But somehow . . . Brother Gilbert doubted it.

Chapter 11

*T*he Way to the Black Bog

By the time Pip got them to the old Roman canal, the sun had already risen, and everyone was desperate to sleep. But Rane would only allow a few hours of rest.

'We have until noon,' she said firmly. 'The next instruction is a bit poetic, but there's no problem understanding what it means. "*Follow the road along the path of the sun, from its strength to mid-way to its rest.*" That's noon till mid-afternoon, going west.'

No one had the courage to suggest waiting until noon the *next* day.

Leaving the canal behind, they struck off at an angle into the hot breathless afternoon, and threaded through a series of islands. *'On the left four and two more on the right like feathers on an arrow that would not fly true.'*

Pip couldn't help noticing the increasingly suspicious looks he was getting. Somehow the twins seemed to blame *him* for Johan Shortleg's loopy directions. But when they were faced with a wonderfully clear stretch of water, and Rane's translation insisted they make an elaborate dog's leg *away* from it, things got even worse. The manuscript led them right into a dense maze of channels and passages and floating islands. With so many detours and backtrackings necessary, it was impossible to tell if they were even going in the right direction anymore. To make things worse, the twins kept complaining that they heard noises, as if they weren't alone out there, as if someone were following them. But neither Pip nor Rane heard anything, so it must have been their imaginations.

They wandered on like that for several hours, when all at once Leif snapped.

'You little . . . Where are you taking us?!' he suddenly started yelling at Pip. 'You've tricked us, haven't you – You've got us lost – I'm going to break every cheating bone in your—' He tried to shove past his brother to get to Pip – and came to within a breath of tipping everyone and everything out of the punt. Rane barked an order, and he managed to restrain himself. He subsided into a grumbling heap in the bottom of the punt.

No more was said, and not long afterwards they finally blundered out of the maze, and were able to make better time on more open water.

But Leif hadn't forgotten. That night they were camped on a bit of ground only slightly drier than the surrounding marsh. Rane was busy poring over her manuscript again, and Olaf was cooking some fish for them to eat. Pip was just sitting in a heap, bone tired and unable to care about anything at all. He didn't pay attention when Leif came over and hunkered down beside him – until the big man began to talk.

'You know,' he said in a husky, menacing whisper, 'our mistress is a lady, and high-born, and a good Christian. There are any number of things it's not fit for her to be seen to do. My brother and I' – and the threatening tone deepened – 'now, *we* are none of those. There really is very little *we* won't do, and we don't mind *who's* watching!' He stood up, still not looking Pip in the eye. 'Just so you know,' he added.

His words confirmed the boy's every fear. As Leif walked away, Pip stared down at his hands. They were shaking.

'This is almost the last instruction,' said Rane the next morning. 'And it's a simple one, for a wonder. "*Make your way due east for the best part of a day.*" No problem interpreting that, at least.' She paused and looked over at Pip. 'What's wrong?'

East. It had to be east – the one direction he'd been dreading!

'I'll tell you what's wrong,' he said drearily. 'Going east will take us right into the Black Bog.'

Rane nodded slowly. 'I see. And that's bad?'

Pip's face was all the answer she needed.

The Black Bog was a part of the Fen that the marsh people kept well away from. They didn't even like to *talk* about it, at least not above a whisper. Pip only knew hints and rumours. He remembered getting a shivery pleasure out of hearing those hints and rumours when he was at home, safe in the Wickit kitchen. He'd actually begged for more!

Now he wished he'd never even *heard* of the place they were heading for. Thoughts of bogles and water-wraiths and the walking, wailing dead battered about in his head.

*Trust that wretched old man to hide his treasure **there***! Pip muttered to himself. He'd developed an enormous dislike for Johan Short-leg almost from the first moment of hearing his name, and this did nothing to change his opinion.

I bet he'd have got on with Prior Benet, he thought, though for some reason the Prior didn't seem quite as gruesome as usual.

They hadn't gone all that far east before the landscape began to change. The reed beds became denser and the water more sluggish. Even the mud seemed different – it clung in black globs to the punt's pole with every stroke, making horrible sucking noises as Pip dragged it out. When he tried to scrape it off on the side of the boat, it left a foul-smelling mess.

As the reeds crowded in, and the air became harder to breathe, everyone became more and more silent and nervous. Every time Pip looked over his shoulder there was nothing to see, but he still felt watched.

The Black Bog did not want them here,

disturbing its creepy, claustrophobic stillness, poking into its secrets.

By midday, they had to leave the punt behind. But, true to Johan's instructions, a path wound away through the reeds, and they were able to continue on an easterly heading.

'Who made this?' Rane asked, her voice sounding unusually subdued. 'Animals?'

Pip shrugged uncertainly. 'Maybe. Maybe not. There are stories of . . . things that live in this part of the Fen.'

'Things?' she said, but Pip didn't want to talk about that.

He took the lead. Rane came next, then the twins followed on, with the contents of the punt divided between them. Nobody said much, other than the occasional muffled curse at the suffocating clouds of biting insects that plagued them. By the time they stopped for the night, everyone was nearly crazy with it all.

As the others shuffled about, half-heartedly making camp, Pip headed back down the path.

'Where do you think you're going?!' snarled Olaf.

Pip slapped irritably at his face. 'Back to where the path widened. There were ferns back there.'

'So? What do you want ferns for?' Olaf's eyes narrowed.

'To put on a fire.'

The big man stared at him, looking stupid and suspicious. 'Ferns? A fire? In this heat?'

'Yes, ferns! Yes, a fire! The smoke will drive the insects off. Unless you *like* being eaten alive.' Pip didn't care how rude he sounded. Just at this moment, biting bugs loomed larger in his mind than bad-tempered Norsemen. 'And there'll be snakes here, too. Snakes *hate* fern smoke. *Everybody* knows that.'

Olaf squinted at him for another moment and then nodded grudgingly. 'But I'm coming with you,' he said.

'You do that,' said Pip.

They brought back armfuls of ferns, and the smudge did help with the bugs. Everyone tried to sit as close to the smoke as they could, in spite of the way it made them cough and their eyes sting. With nightfall, the air became a little cooler, and the merest whisper of a breeze let the weary humans sleep . . .

It was the dark hour before dawn when Olaf suddenly sat up. He peered about groggily, wondering what had woken him . . . when he heard it again. He reached across and shook his brother by the shoulder.

'Leif!' he whispered. 'What's that?!'

'Huh?' Leif was never at his best on first waking, especially when you woke him before the normal time. Olaf just shook him harder.

'That *sound* – what is it?!'

'It's nothing. I didn't hear anything. It's just an animal,' Leif mumbled.

'How can it be just an animal if you didn't hear anything?!' snapped Olaf.

Leif realised he was not going to get back to sleep without some kind of effort. He sat up, and made a show of listening to the sounds of the night with great care.

'Well,' he said at last, 'whatever it was, it's gone now.'

'Are you sure?' asked Olaf anxiously.

Leif nodded in the dark.

'Of course I'm sure. You can go to sleep now.'

Olaf was reassured by his twin's confidence, and lay down.

Soon, the only sound to be heard was the snores of the sleepers.

And when a branch shifted a little on the fire and flared up, no one noticed the glint of eyes, watching from the shelter of the reeds.

Chapter 12

Mire!

No one had much to say to each other as they broke camp the next morning. They were all too tired, and too keyed-up, and the end of all the effort was too close.

Pip led the way, with Perfect hidden away inside his hood. Her face jutted out a little from behind his left ear, so she could see where they were going. With all the sleep she'd been getting on this trip, she was quite chirpy and alert, but the rest of them were walking in a daze, thinking of nothing, just putting one foot in front of the other. After a while, the path widened out, and acquired a covering of nice green plants of some sort—

'*STOP!!*'

Perfect's squeal nearly deafened Pip, and everybody jumped and bumped into each other.

'What?!'

'Who said that?!'

'Eh?!'

Pip cleared his throat and tried to not look so startled himself. 'I – it was me,' he stuttered, 'and the reason I yelled "Stop!" was . . .'

And then he saw it. It was right in front of them, as innocent-looking as a hillside meadow and as lethal as a poisonous snake.

'Quagmire,' Pip finished, his voice shaking slightly. 'From here right to where the path narrows again, way over there.'

No one seemed to understand. Rane tried to push past him.

'What are you talking about? I can't see anything. What's quagmire?'

Pip's answer sounded angry but it was really fear they heard in his voice. 'It's sucking bog!' he snapped. 'Like quicksand, only wetter! It's death by suffocation, if you must know, and we very nearly walked straight into it. We have to go back. There's no way forward through quagmire!'

'I don't know . . .' Perfect whispered. He could hear her sniffing hard. 'It just might support *your* weight. Or the girl's. If you were quick enough. But it *certainly* wouldn't support those other two. Much too fat.'

Rane had been eavesdropping shamelessly. 'So *we* could get across – or Pip, couldn't we just go *around* it?'

'It's not safe going off the path, even if we could cut a way through the reeds,' he said. 'There's no telling what will suddenly be underfoot.'

Rane nodded absently, as if she already knew he would say that.

'It's too much of a risk – we have to go back,' he said urgently, reaching out a hand. But she was too fast for him. She slipped out from under his grasp and without a word, darted out onto the surface of the mire.

As the others watched in horror, she ran quickly across the surface, light as a cat. Even so, she set the mud below the green lolloping. Hungry slurping noises escaped from the edges. Then she was across, panting with excitement, to the place where the ground was solid again.

'Now you, Pip!' Rane gasped, holding out

her hands. 'Don't think about it – just *run!*'

The last thing on earth Pip wanted to do was to trust himself to that evilly-pretty expanse of green, but he couldn't disobey . . .

He ran, as if the dead hands of the marsh were reaching up to grab him by the ankles as he passed. But still the surface held, even though it undulated in sinister waves. He caught Rane's outstretched hands and collapsed onto solid ground, shaking with relief.

'Now me!' yelled Olaf – and before Pip could tell him no, he was too heavy, the surface would never support him – he had lumbered forward. One step, two steps, five, six . . . a look of triumph was just starting to spread across his face when, without warning, the surface green opened up and the black mud dragged him down. It was so fast – he was submerged to his waist before anyone had really understood what was happening. A wave of stink burped up from the black goo. Olaf's first reaction was to bellow and thrash, which sank him even further. The mire was to his chest now. Some ancient instinct kicked in, and he froze, arms spread, his eyes showing white all the way round like a spooked horse.

Leif was frantic.

'Olaf! Olaf!!' he roared.

'What can we do?!' Rane cried. Pip spun round, looking about desperately, but there was nothing on their side of the mire that would reach so far. Then he saw it – the punt pole, unnoticed on the ground beside Leif.

'Use the pole!' Pip yelled.

Leif looked about wildly, unable to see anything clearly.

'There – *there* – by your feet!' Rane and Pip pointed and shrieked.

Leif lifted his feet up in a frantic dance, located the pole and wrenched it out of the soft ground. With a bellow he pivoted the length of wood over-arm and whacked it onto the bog, narrowly missing his brother's head.

Pip and Rane clung to each other, hardly daring to breathe, as Olaf's flailing hands found the pole.

Immediately Leif heaved hard, but his brother's hands were slick with muck and the pole shot out between them. Leif landed on his back with a squawk of panic.

'Try again!' Rane croaked.

'Slowly – *gently*,' Pip pleaded.

With exaggerated care, Leif laid the pole alongside his brother again.

'Let him come to you!' Pip called, and Leif nodded. He planted his feet firmly and leaned back, while Olaf, grunting like an ox at the plough, clawed himself along the pole towards safety.

It seemed to take forever. Then, at last, stinking and slick with muck, Olaf crawled out of the quagmire and back onto solid ground. Leif dropped the pole and collapsed beside him. The two grinned at each other like idiots, giving each other relieved punches and pats. Finally they calmed down.

'You'll have to go on without us, Lady!' Leif called across to Rane.

'Told you,' Perfect murmured.

'Wait for me, then,' Rane called back. Then she whispered to the dragon, 'Stay alert, Perfect! Your nose will keep us safe.'

'Still east?' Pip asked.

Rane nodded. '*And east to the harvest of stones.* That's the very last thing that's written.' She looked at him, wide-eyed. 'We're nearly there.'

Pip groaned. 'God's Eyebrows – not another riddle!'

Rane shrugged. Perfect and Pip both kept a sharp lookout, but it seemed as if the stretch of quagmire was the last thing the Black Bog had left to throw at them. The path became drier and easier to walk on, and the land rose gently above the level of the reeds until they reached a strange open space. They came to a halt, and stared.

'A *harvest of stones*,' murmured Rane. Pip could only nod.

Low scrub surrounded a roughly circular area that was planted with slabs of stone. They were different sizes, ranging from half a metre tall to close to two. Some were standing upright, others had fallen over, some leaned against the neighbours like tired friends. They were all roughly rectangular, and they all must have been brought here by someone, for no rock like this was native to the bog landscape.

'Who . . .?' Rane began, but Pip shook his head. It wasn't good to talk about such things, not in such a place. Rane didn't argue.

'Johan will have buried his Hoard at the edge, I think, so as not to disturb . . . anyone,' she said in a quiet voice. 'Come on.'

She started to turn right and then abruptly swung round and headed left. Pip approved. It was always wise to go clockwise – some called it sun-wise – round anything even remotely super-natural. Even so, he was intensely grateful when she stopped again almost immediately and dropped to her knees.

'There!' she breathed. 'Look there!'

Johan Shortleg had brought a stone of his own to the harvest. His was a piece of slate and it had a marking scratched on it like the ones on the manuscript.

'What does it mean?' Pip whispered.

Rane drew a deep breath. 'It means *"Here"*,' she said and, pulling out her dagger, she began to dig.

She hadn't far to go. Barely five inches below the surface, her blade scraped on more slate. Johan had made a small stone-lined chamber for his Hoard, to protect it from water damage and subsidence. Rane loosened the top slab and, with Pip's help, lifted it away. Then, together, they eased the box that was inside out of the ground and into the daylight.

For a long moment, the three of them stared down at the dirty, scuffed-up box and were afraid. Afraid of what they might find – and even more afraid of what they might not find – when they opened it. The wind had dropped and everything was strangely quiet, so that it was as if a circle of silence had formed with the mud-stained, bedraggled little group at its centre.

It was Perfect who broke the spell.

'Open it, Lady,' she said in a gentle voice. 'It's why you came.'

Rane took a ragged breath and nodded. Without taking her eyes off the box, she cleaned the blade of her knife on the skirt of her gown, and slid it carefully under the edge of the lid. She worked it slowly along until it reached the lock, then she levered upwards until the rusted mechanism gave with a dull snap. She withdrew the blade, laid the knife aside, and lifted the lid.

It came away easily, almost gratefully, in her hands. Three heads craned forward to see what was inside, and three mouths went round in wonder.

'Well, my goodness gracious me,' said Perfect – and no one disagreed.

Chapter 13

Johan's Legacy

The box was full of gold. Twisted gold bracelets, gold rings, gold torcs with dragon's heads, gold brooches covered in intricate golden designs . . .

One of Rane's braids fell forward over her shoulder. As it lay across the heap of jewels, it blended in, as if it had been part of the treasure all along.

'From the beginning, the people of the North have had a love affair with silver. But for my family, it has always been gold . . .' She looked over at Pip and smiled.

'Is there enough – there *must* be enough?!' Pip asked.

'Enough and to spare,' Rane murmured,

stroking a torc lovingly, as if it were a cat or a child. 'Here – try these on for size!' And she shoved two bracelets and a bevy of rings at Pip. Soon they were both dressed up to the eyebrows in jewellery, laughing and delighted, giddy with their success. The sun glinted crazily off them as they waved their arms about and danced round the box.

'There must be enough gold here to sink a ship!' Pip flopped down at last, out of breath, and grinned over at Rane. The grin froze on his face as he caught sight of the expression on hers.

'What is it?' he whispered.

She dropped down beside him. 'Listen to yourself – *enough gold to sink a ship* – how heavy do you think that makes it? . . . *How are we going to get it across the mire?!*'

They stared at each other in horror.

'How am I going to get the box across?' Rane repeated. 'If I try to carry it, won't I be too heavy? Won't I sink, the way Olaf did?'

Pip could see it as clearly as if it were happening in front of him there and then – Rane, laden down with golden bracelets and necklaces and rings and clutching the box in her arms, sliding out of sight below that green deceptive surface . . .

'But if we can't carry it across . . .?'

He was so tired now, it was getting harder and harder to think. *We **can't** have come through all this for nothing*, Pip thought, *we **can't** have!* He didn't even notice he was saying 'we'.

'Leave the box,' came a voice. 'And let me do it.'

'What?'

He looked round and there was Perfect. She had three bracelets hanging round her neck and a dozen rings decorated her tail. And she had a determined expression on her little stone face.

'*What?!*'

'I think it would work.' The two humans stared at her, but in spite of the unlikely getup, she didn't *look* as if she'd gone mad. 'What we'll do is this. You, Pip, you take a good run up, right, and get me launched. Give it all you've got. I'll be wearing as much gold as I can, and you throw me, as hard as *you* can, and I flap as hard as *I* can . . .'

'Like a spear with wings . . . ' Rane murmured.

'I get to the other side. I take off the rings and things, give them to the yellow-haired fellows to look after, get them to toss me back . . . '

'Then we load you up, and do it again!'

'Back and forth until we've got it all across—'

'Then, quick as rabbits and light as anything, the mere human types run across and everybody gets reunited!'

'Of course they'll have to see me.'

There was a horrified pause as they realised what Perfect was saying.

'I gave you my word . . .' said Rane. 'I said I wouldn't let anyone know.'

'That's all right.' The little dragon puffed up her stony chest and tried to look big. 'They don't bother *me*.'

'That's my brave girl!' Rane cried, with a crazy glint in her eye. 'But I'll tell you something for nothing – I can positively guarantee that *you're* going to bother *them*!'

Chapter 14

Flying Dragons!

If the whole situation hadn't been so dangerous, Pip would have thoroughly enjoyed watching the twins from Helheim trying to catch, unload, and then re-launch Perfect without actually looking at her. Rane had shown the dragon to them from the far side of the quagmire, introducing her as a child of the World Serpent, and they knew at once that they were in the presence of something so far out of the ordinary it made their brains bubble. Eventually, however, they seem to decide that if they didn't look at Perfect directly – or even better, if they didn't look at her at all! – then maybe she wasn't really there. Or maybe if *they* didn't see *her*, *she* wouldn't see *them*? Or maybe . . .

They got so they couldn't look at each other, either, and kept banging heads as they packed up the box they'd carried with them from the punt with the rings and bracelets and torcs.

Perfect flew as if her life depended on it – and if she had landed short on any of her loaded trips across the sucking bog, that would have been no less than the truth. By the end, Pip was frantic about how tired she was getting, and the last trip was more of an out-of-control glide than a proper flight.

And then, finally, it was over. Perfect lay in an exhausted heap as Olaf and Leif took the last of the jewellery from around her neck. Laughing with relief, Rane dashed lightly across the quivering bog to make much of her.

Pip let the sinister lolloping of the surface calm down before following. As he waited, he took one last look around to make sure no fragment of the treasure had fallen unnoticed to the ground. The box that had kept the old Viking's Hoard safe for so long lay on its side, empty and forlorn, there at his feet where they'd dropped it. Something made him lean over and straighten it now, closing the lid and brushing the dirt off with a gentle hand. For a brief moment he felt a connection across the years with Johan, who had handled this same box, filled it with golden treasure, and entrusted it with his family's future.

Then the moment passed. Pip, smiling a little at himself and his fancy, straightened up, turned to go – and froze, struck speechless by what was happening right then, right in front of him, on the other side of the mire.

Perfect had vanished. Olaf and Leif were backed up almost into the sucking bog, on their knees with their hands in the air. Like Pip, they seemed frozen, their attention fixed absolutely on the ghostly, ghastly apparition that had appeared before them. For a moment, Pip didn't recognize the figure either, even though he'd tended to him in the Infirmary all those days and nights.

And then he realised who it was . . .

Cedric, the King's man, was in a terrible state. He was caked in mud to the thighs and his face and hands were badly bitten by insects. It looked as if his fever might be coming back too, for he was starting to shake again. (Pip could have told him as much – his illness was one that could easily return if enough care wasn't taken.)

But in spite of all that, he had a tight, grim

115

little smile on his face. Whatever mess he was in, they were in worse – for Cedric had the box of gold at his feet. He also had the Lady Rane, her arms pinned behind her and an unsheathed dagger to her throat.

Pip's mind seemed to be a sea of treacle. He didn't know what to do – he couldn't think of anything *to* do. He just stood there, looking stupid, helpless, hopeless . . . . The smile on Cedric's face deepened.

Then, without warning, Perfect launched herself at him from the reeds, screaming in a way Pip had never heard before, her stone claws outstretched and her sharp little stone teeth revealed. She aimed straight for Cedric's dagger hand. He shrieked and dropped the blade, losing his grip on Rane and clutching his bleeding hand to himself . . .

. . . before toppling face-forward into the mud!

Pip gulped, unable to believe what he was seeing. There, standing behind the fallen King's man, was Haakon, a log of wood hanging from his hand. He'd hit Cedric across the back of the head with it, and knocked him cold.

He held out his arm and clucked, and Perfect leaped up onto it, clinging to his sleeve like a bird of prey. The old man seemed completely unfazed by his supernatural battle companion. For one horrible moment, as they stared triumphantly at each other, Pip forgot everything else – Rane, the gold, Cedric – and could only yell inside his head, *She's mine! Put her down! Let go of her!*

Then as Rane rushed over to the old man, Perfect hopped off his arm, looked across the mire to Pip, and grinned with love in her eyes.

It was all right. It was going to be fine.

As Pip made his last run across the deceptive greenness, Rane was already regaining her own equanimity. She let the old man go, stepped back, and dropped him a deep, formal curtsey, paying no heed to the mud.

'Kinsman,' she said with barely a wobble in her voice, 'I owe you my life.'

Haakon bowed solemnly and then, with a grin, turned suddenly to the twins, still kneeling, their mouths hanging open in astonishment.

'Not such a waste of time *now*, am I? Eh? Eh?' he bellowed at them as they struggled to their feet. The embarrassed confusion on their faces made a picture the old man would cherish for years to come – and Pip got a fair amount of pleasure out of it too! Haakon explained in a loud, proud voice how he had trailed the King's man all the way from Wickit without being discovered, ready at any time to come to the rescue when the felon made his move . . .

Pip smiled. It was a story that would no doubt grow with every telling. He went over to Perfect and picked her up.

'Are you all right?' he murmured as he looked her over and then slid her over his shoulder into his hood. 'Did you hurt yourself at all?'

He heard a tiny yawn. 'No problem,' she whispered back. 'It was a doddle. But I think, if no one needs me for the next little while . . .' Another yawn was followed almost at once by the reassuring buzz of a Perfect snore.

When he turned back to them, he saw that the Norse party was preparing to leave. Olaf held the box of gold with great care and concentration. Leif was trying to stay as far away from Haakon as space allowed, and the old man was busy looking enormously smug. Rane gestured happily to Pip to come and lead the way back. None of them was paying any attention to the crumpled Cedric lying, still unconscious, in the mud.

'But just a minute!' Pip protested. 'What about *him*?!'

'Leave him,' grunted Olaf.

'No, slit his throat first and *then* leave him,' said Leif.

Haakon just shrugged.

Horrified, Pip turned to Rane – and was appalled to see how *un*appalled *she* looked. This was exactly what he'd feared for himself!

'You *can't* . . .!' he squeaked.

'I suppose not,' she agreed reluctantly. 'But I'm not carting him all the way back to Wickit – and I'm *certainly* not taking him *home* with me!'

Pip realised everyone was looking at him, expecting him to tell them what they *could* do with Cedric.

'Don't worry – I'll think of something,' he said, and hoped to goodness he would!

Chapter 15

Sly and the Ghosts

Sly the Fisherman sometimes went for years without seeing a ghost, but this summer they seemed to be popping up everywhere. He wondered if it had something to do with the especially hot weather, but he didn't remember that happening in hot summers before. *This* time, though, they'd been stranger even than usual. For one thing, they'd come right up to his hut in broad daylight. *And* they'd had a ghost with them who looked just like the boy from Wickit. *And* they'd given him gold . . .

Ghost-gold! He let the punt glide for a moment and felt in his pouch one more time, just to be sure the coins hadn't vanished. No, they were still there. Two gold coins that clinked together in a very exciting way. One gold coin just for going to Ely – which he'd planned to do anyway, with eels to sell – taking the sick man with him, and another gold coin just for not talking about them when he got there. As if he would! *Everybody* knew it was bad luck to talk about *ordinary* ghosts, and to talk about ghosts who gave you gold . . . well, that would be just plain stupid.

As the sick man slept peacefully, there in the bottom of the punt amongst the eel baskets, Fisher Sly congratulated himself on *not* being stupid, and poled off towards Ely with renewed energy and an expression of smug satisfaction all over his face.

Chapter 16

My Mountains . . .

The journey from the Black Bog to the coast passed without disaster. Pip had sworn to get Rane and her treasure safely back to her ship, and it looked as if he were going to do just that. He should have felt happy and relieved.

But he didn't. If the truth be told, he felt lonely.

Haakon was too exhausted by the ordeal of trailing Cedric across the marshland to talk to him, and spent most of his time asleep in the bottom of one of the punts. (They had three now, the Norse boat, and the two stolen from the monastery.) Olaf and Leif were no longer willing to even acknowledge Pip's *existence*, since the handler of the child of the World Serpent was like her in not being *safe*. They kept their distance when they could and looked away whenever he was near.

Neither Rane nor Perfect were much company either. Whenever the gargoyle wasn't asleep, he would see them deep in talk together, the little dragon perched attentively on her knee. It seemed as if they were always doing that, whenever Pip looked around. He watched them from the stern of the punt, and tried to ignore the hard horrible knot of jealousy in his stomach.

They arrived at last at the sea, at the meeting place, on a fine, balmy morning. The men stayed by the punts, silent and suddenly anxious. Rane walked with Pip and Perfect down to the edge of the shingle and stood, staring out to sea. She too was quiet for a while, but then she turned and spoke directly to the gargoyle, perched on Pip's shoulder.

'Of course, if you came with me you wouldn't *have* to hide,' Rane said. It was as if she were simply carrying on with one of a hundred conversations she and Perfect had had. *Now* Pip knew what they had been talking about all those times before, when they'd looked so solemnly at each other, and whispered so earnestly. '*My* people would know how to respect a child of the World Serpent. They would fear you, and honour you, as you deserve.' Her pale blue eyes fixed Perfect to the spot, as unblinking as if she were a gargoyle herself. It was that gaze almost more than the words that seemed to be hypnotising the little dragon.

Pip could hardly breathe.

'And the mountains . . . until you have seen my mountains, you are only half alive – so tall the snow stays on the high places right through the summer, then a straight plunge down to the slate blue water of the fjords and on down after that. They say my mountains have their feet in the heart of the world, and when they wiggle their toes, towns shake a thousand miles away! Your air, here, it is like breathing soup – it leaves you only half awake – but when you breathe in the wind from my mountains or the wind from the sea, you want to run and jump and shout.' She smiled at Perfect. 'Or fly . . . Can't you see it? Can't you imagine?'

And Perfect *could* imagine it – Pip could see she could, and in spite of everything, he found he couldn't blame her. It sounded so blue and white and wonderful and—

'I told you – I'd never go anywhere without Pip.'

Perfect sounded completely calm and matter-of-fact, as if they were discussing nothing more than the weather. Pip's brain reeled. Were they talking about what he thought they were talking about? Were they talking about him leaving the Fens – going away? That was crazy! How could he ever go *away*?

There was a thoughtful look on Rane's face. She nodded slowly and was about to speak, when Leif suddenly cried out to them,

'Lady! Look – there she is!!'

The longboat slid out of the inlet, lean as a predator, soft as a whisper, and for a moment Pip felt an old, old fear shudder in him. It was as if some part of him *remembered* the hundreds of years of coastal terror. Every spring, just as winter's stranglehold eased, the raiders came over the sea with the torch and the sword, and flavoured the season of new hope with dread. Pip had never known those times, nor had his parents, nor theirs, but still some part of him recognized the shape of death in the dawn.

Then Rane spoke, and the memory evaporated.

'Beautiful, isn't she?' she said quietly, and Pip saw that it was true.

Leif and Olaf were leaping about on the shore like mad things, frantic to be on proper water again and on their way home. Haakon was smiling benignly and Rane – Rane was aglow with delight and pride. Pip had never seen her more beautiful.

She swung round to face them, laughing and excited, and said, 'Well, are you coming? Both of you? Are you coming with me?'

And at that moment, neither Perfect nor Pip could see how they could possibly say no.

It took no time at all to load the longboat. The tide was on the turn, and the ship seemed eager to be on its way, tugging at the mooring ropes and bobbing on the waves. Then, without a backward glance, they were away, free, moving off into the low-lying off-shore fog at a good speed.

For a time the mist was all there was to see. Then the sun broke through, and the longboat showed itself, far out on the water and drenched in yellow light. It was as if all the gold in all the world had been hammered out thin, and wrapped round Rane's ship, so that it had become a ransom fit for the gods. Just for a moment. Then the mist swirled round again, and there was only greyness left.

Chapter 17

What the Abbot Saw

Abbot Michael was troubled.

It had been muggy and hot in the night again, with no breeze to move the heavy air about. The day looked set for more of the same – another scorcher – and, not for the first time this difficult summer, Abbot Michael thought longingly of the cool, damp greenness of Wales. He got up and prayed for a moment. Then, with a sigh, he went to the window. As he looked out, his eyes were full of memory, of the high hills he grew up among, of the way the cries of the sheep carried across the valleys in the clear air, of the . . .

'What's that?' he murmured, frowning.

The rising sun hitting the water made it glint painfully but there appeared to be something coming, straight out of the east – something that had nothing to do with green hills, or his childhood.

Suddenly Abbot's frown blossomed into a smile of delight.

'*Pip!*' His voice rang out from the Abbey to the shore. It was the boy. He'd come back! There was a flurry of activity and some splashing – it was almost as if part of the front of the punt had suddenly fallen into the water. Not that it mattered! A new punt would be a small price to pay . . . 'Wait there!' he called out. 'Don't move!'

'He came back,' the Abbot murmured contentedly to himself as he hurried out of his room. 'He came back.'

On the shore, Pip helped Perfect climb back into the punt.

'Did he see me?' she asked anxiously. 'Do you think he could see me?'

Pip pulled the second punt they'd been towing up beside the first and moored it safely. Then he gave her a quick reassuring rubdown and tucked her into his shirt.

'I'm pretty sure he didn't,' he said

nervously. 'He was looking into the sun – he shouldn't have been able to distinguish details against the glare.'

'Ooo, so now I'm just a *detail*?!' Perfect slid down his sleeve, stuck out her head and looked sideways up at him. 'Maybe I *should* have gone with the girl to her country – I'd be more than just a detail *there!*'

Pip looked stricken. 'Oh Perfect,' he cried. 'You gave up all that respect and you'd never have to hide again and, and— '

Then he stopped in mid-word. 'What are you laughing at?' he asked suspiciously.

'At you, of course!' the little dragon snickered. 'For being so thick. Don't you understand – the hiding's the second best part of everything!'

'It is? Then what's the best part of everything?'

Perfect pulled her head back into his sleeve just as the Abbot began to jog joyfully across the foreshore towards them.

'You,' she said.

The World of Wickit

(stranger than fiction, weirder than fantasy)

The Keeper of the Wickit Chronicles
Answers Your Questions

How do you make a sign against the evil eye?

To protect yourself against demons and the evil eye, place your thumb between your index and middle finger while making a fist.

Did people get headaches that long ago?

I think it's pretty safe to say that as long as there have been heads, there have been headaches. Brother Gilbert tended towards lovely smelling ingredients in *his* headache remedies, like lavender or roses, but he could just as easily have chosen to use the seeds of the skullcap plant. This is because, if you looked at them just right, the seeds look like little skulls. According to the Doctrine of Signatures, this meant that God, who had provided help for every illness in the world, had marked those seeds out as being good for head pain. This could be applied to all sorts of things – liverwort leaves were thought to look like livers, so the plant was used to treat liver ailments; the maidenhair fern was thought to help baldness; toothwort has lots of leaves that look a bit like – yes, you guessed it – teeth, and was used for toothache, and so on. Remedies for illnesses were everywhere.

You just had to have rather peculiar eyesight in order to see them.

Why did Brother Gilbert have a bunch of willow tree branches in his Infirmary?

The willow grows in cool watery places and is associated with the moon which mostly comes out in the cool of the night, so branches of it were thought to be good for bringing down fever in a patient. Pip was giving Cedric a sedative to help him sleep, but the drink would most likely also have included willow bark. This contains a bitter-tasting substance called salicin, very similar to the man-made painkiller, aspirin.

What's ague?

What Pip's time called ague was in fact malaria. And you could still catch malaria in Britain if you lived in a swampy, mosquito-ridden part right up until the First World War. Brother Gilbert would have made use of a number of remedies to bring down the fever and ease the pain of the headache, such as coltsfoot, anise, valerian and yarrow. If none of those worked, though, he might have got desperate

and tried one of the slightly weirder
cures – like getting Haakon to swallow
a spider shoved inside a raisin . . .

*Where's Helheim, and why is it rude to
be said to come from there? And who's
Loki? And what's this World Serpent Perfect's supposed to be related to?*

Haakon had really had it with Leif
and Olaf, and calling them rude names
made him feel better. In Norse
mythology, Helheim was the home of the
dishonoured dead – the ones who didn't
get to go to Valhalla because they didn't
die gloriously in battle. It was located
on the lowest level of the Norse
universe. The goddess in charge of

Helheim was called Hel. So every time somebody now says 'Oh, Hell!' they're invoking a Norse goddess. This can be a bad idea.

Loki, for example, was the Norse god of mischief. He had many other names – the Sly One, the Trickster, the Shape Changer. He was notoriously unreliable and never forgot a slight. He also had a large number of peculiar children. Hel, in fact, was a daughter of his, as was Jormungand, the World Serpent, who was so large he could wrap himself right round the world and bite his own tail. Why he would *want* to do this is not known. Calling Perfect a child of the World Serpent was just Rane's way of giving the twins some way of understanding her – wisely, she didn't want two guys as big as that completely freaking out.

Why was Rane's ancestor called John Shortleg – what kind of a surname is that?

The Vikings didn't use surnames in quite the way we do, but they were keen on nicknames, which helped them tell people with the same first names apart. Some of them are self-explanatory: Erik Bloodaxe, for example, or Harald Fairhair. Women could also acquire nicknames if they were high-class enough. There was Aud the Deep-Minded, a very clever and able woman, or the princess Ragnhild the Mighty. Some other ones I particularly like are Harald Bluetooth, Ketil Flat-Nose, and Rolf the Ganger. 'Ganger' means 'Walker' – the man was so fat no horse could carry him, so he *had* to walk.

What's a rune?

Runes were the Norse equivalent of an alphabet. They were made up of combinations of straight lines, which made them easy to carve on stone. They looked like this:

What's apoplexy?

Apoplexy was the medieval word for a stroke. Brother Gilbert would probably have prescribed a decoction of lavender, horehound, fennel and asparagus roots, with a touch of cinnamon, for Rane's father, though some physicians preferred to hang sprigs of mistletoe round the stroke victim's neck.

What's a debt-thrall?

There were different degrees of serfdom in Norse society, but to become a debt-thrall – to be sold into slavery because you couldn't pay your debts – was considered a particularly shameful way to lose your freedom. Rane wouldn't really be selling herself into slavery, but if she were to go to a husband with only a cancelled debt as her dowry, she would be giving up an important part of her status and independence as a married woman. The dowry or bride money belonged to the bride, and if she decided to divorce her husband, he had to pay her the money back. If Rane wanted out of her marriage, though, all *she* would get would be the huge debt back, and still no way of paying it.

What kind of church has dragons on the roof?

The Norse were good at finding room for more than one religion at a time, and Christian and pagan things were often found quite comfortably side by side. Like the fabulous wooden stave church in Norway with the dragons on the roof that Rane mentions to Perfect. (Strangely, it looks a lot like a pagoda!) Or the jeweller's mould which archaeologists found for making amulets. It had holes for pouring molten metal into – in the ▆▆▆▆ape of both the Christian cross *and* Thor's hammer. There may not be a saying in Norse that means 'to hedge your bets', but there should have been.

The World of Wickit . . . like it says on the label, stranger than fiction, weirder than fantasy!

sh